Paul Needs Specs

For Nicola, BC
For Hayley and Harry, GK

First American Edition 2004
by Kane/Miller Book Publishers, Inc.
La Jolla, California

First published by Penguin Books Australia, 2002
Text copyright © Bernard Cohen, 2003
Illustrations copyright © Geoff Kelly, 2003

Library of Congress Control Number: 2003109285

Printed and Bound in China by Regent Publishing Services Ltd.

1 2 3 4 5 6 7 8 9 10

ISBN 1-929132-61-1

Paul Needs Specs

written by

pictures by

Bernard Cohen

Geoff Kelly

Kane/Miller
BOOK PUBLISHERS

Hi.

My name is **Sally.** I'm going to tell you a story about my brother.

My brother's name is Paul. He's hiding. I'm going to tell you why.

Slowly, slowly,

over a very long time,

about a year or even more,

Paul began to notice something

strange.

Everything in his room seemed

to be getting just a little

bit fuzzy.

Some things also seemed a little

bit blurry.

"How odd," thought my brother.

Before now, everything had been

so clear.

He went outside and the
day was **misty**.
He came back inside and the room
was **foggy**.
My brother often had
small accidents.

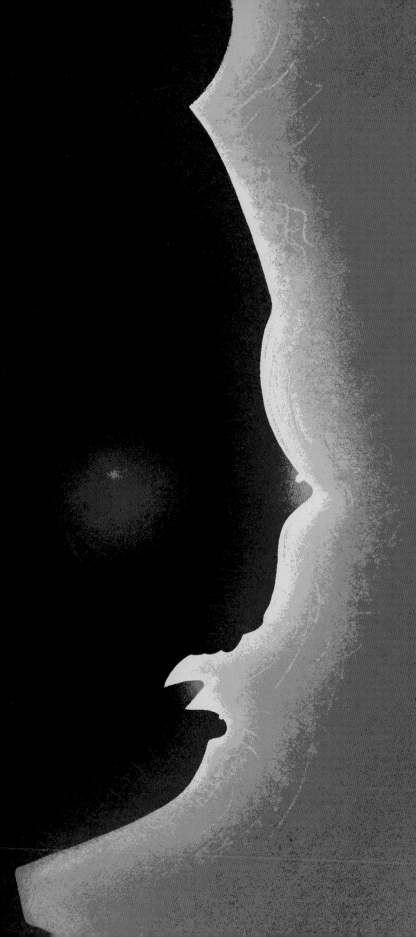

He **bumped**
into his door.

He **tripped**
over his toys.

He **dropped** balls.

He **spilled** his milk.
Paul was so upset
that he cried.

He even asked me about it.

Paul asked, "Has the
world gone **fuzzy**, Sal?"

"Nah" I said.
"It's probably your eyes."

"Do you think so?"
my brother asked.

"Yeah," I said. "Maybe
you need **glasses**."

"Oh," he said.

So Paul and I went to the eye doctor.

The eye doctor tried **all sorts** of lenses on my brother.

Some of them made
him see like this.

And

some

made

him

see

like

this.

And Paul said that **some** even made him see like this.

Hmmm.

But I'm not sure I believe that.

The eye doctor wrote a prescription for the lenses to help Paul see **better.**

Next, we went
to the optician's,
where they sell **glasses**.

The whole shop was full of frames.

Paul chose the ones that suited him **best.**

When the glasses were ready we picked them up.

Then Paul put his new glasses on.

Paul thought the little **lumps** in the road were **really** **very big lumps,** so he tried to step over them.

I laughed a little bit.

Well...a lot really.

And now Paul has glasses.

Nothing is fuzzy or blurry.

Everything he sees is clear.

But Paul is hiding because he thinks
I'll tease him.

I don't want to tease him.

I just want to show you

Paul's new specs.

Paul is hiding.

Come on.
Let's **sneak up**
on him.

We'll **shuffffle**
round here

and **cra~~l**
under this.

We'll t_ipt_oe over here.

And then we'll ju_mp out.

Whoooooooo

Paul's a bit **cross.**

But as you can see,

the specs look good.

And I'm his sister, so I should know.

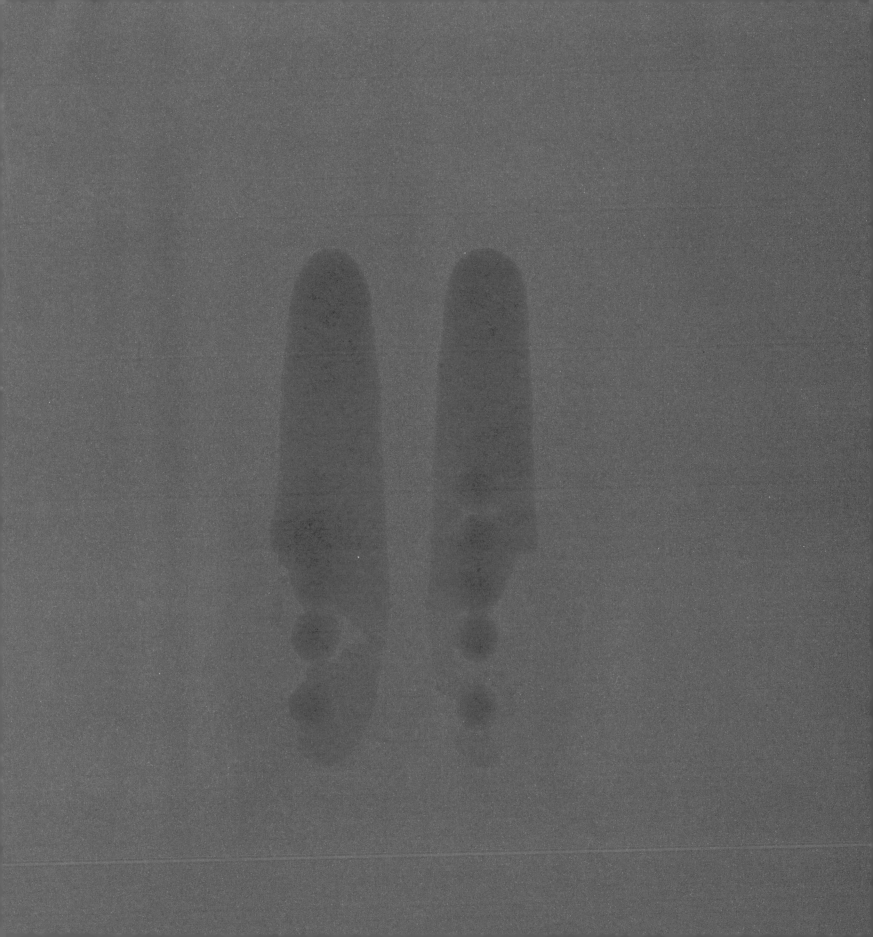

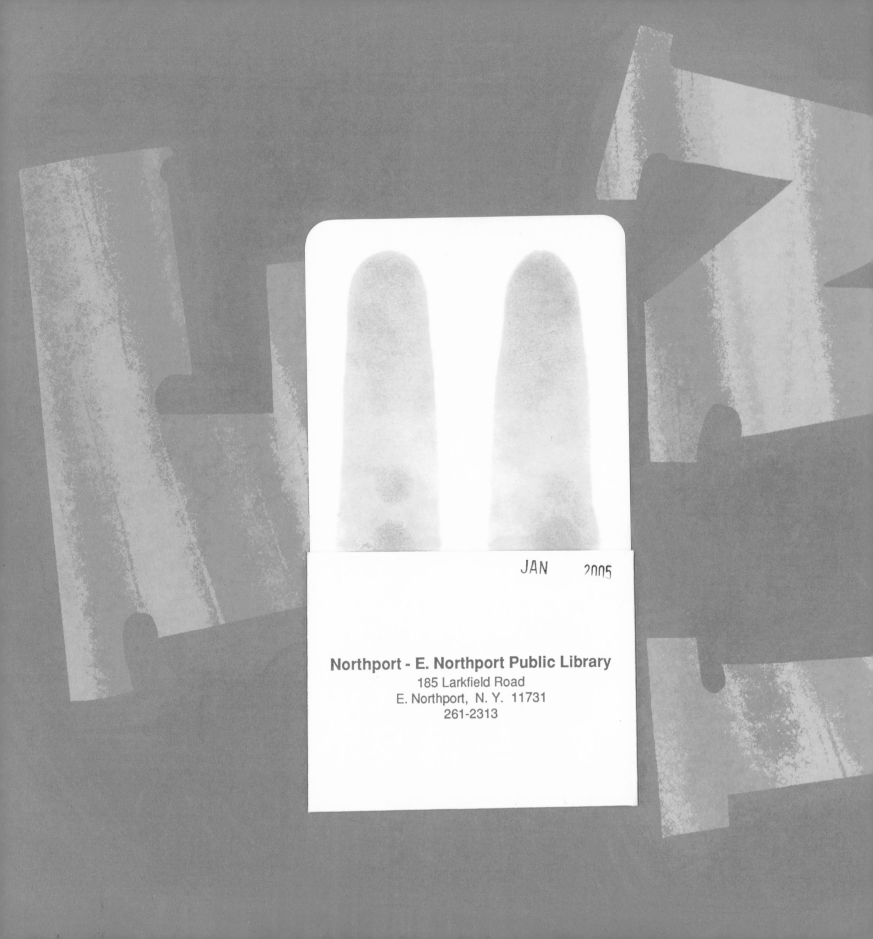